"Colors of Love"

Copyright © 1999 by Billy Bee Productions, Inc.
Published by: Billy Bee Productions, Inc.
P.O. Box 7234 Nashua NH 03060-7234

Library of Congress Catalog Card Number: 99-073484
Library of Congress Cataloging-in-Publication Data
Main entry under title: The Adventures of Billy Bee
Subtitle: Colors of Love
Children's Fiction /Love/Friends/Self Belief/
Author, Peter Thomas
Illustrator John Mahomet
First Edition   10 9 8 7 6 5 4 3 2 1
Printed in Singapore   ISBN 1-886919-11-9

Billy Bee Productions

IT'S TIME TO BEELIEVE!

With greatful acknowledgment to:

God for everything.

My mother and father, Sandra and Henry, for all their unconditional love and support throughout the years and for planting all those very important seeds.

My other mother and father, Ginetta and Emilio, for believing in me enough to help us bring all our dreams to life. It's so wonderful when dreams come true.

To my Uncle Tom Spartichino and Uncle George Spartichino, two great men in my life who knew what I had inside even before I did. I'll never forget that.

The Bitsack's Ned, Diane, Nicole and Alyssa, whenever I think of your wonderful family, it puts a great big smile on my face.

John Mahomet, or should I say, "then along came John." Thank you so much for the wonderful world you have created for Billy Bee, he is as happy as I am.
YOU ARE THE BEST!

Paul Poisson, for always being there. It's always You and I at the end Paul. You are a true credit to your profession and a true friend to have in our life. YOU ARE ALSO THE BEST!

To my Aunt Katherine Maclean, for her valued input. Thank you so much for being there when I needed you Aunt Kathy.

To Karen Gagnon for the fantastic effort she contributed. We are all so very greatful for those wonderful finishing touches.

To Sonya Cutson for helping us to set it all free. Thank you so much Sonya for being here on this wonderful adventure.

To Gilda my beautiful wife,
who has showed me the real meaning of love. It is such a wonderful experience to go through life with you; I am greatful beyond words. It's all because of you Gilda.
I love you so very much, Gillie.
Or should I say Jolly Jillie!

Now everyone get ready because it's

TIME TO BEELIEVE!

I would like to dedicate this book to LOVE.
May you find it everywhere you go,
in everyone you meet
and in everything you do,
but most of all, I hope you LOVE this book :-)

**Billy Bee was outside walking
on a bright clear autumn day,
and as he looked at all the colors,
it nearly took his breath away.**

**The sun was brightly shining
as its golden rays fell down.
It seemed to light up all the flowers
that were scattered on the ground.**

3

There were purple ones and green ones,
some were pink and some were blue,
there were red ones, black and white ones,
some were striped and spotted, too.

The grass was golden yellow
and the hills rolled on forever,
and the sunshine made them glow
like a pirate's sunken treasure.

**Through the middle of it all,
ran a crystal clear blue river
and as the water danced around the rocks,
it seemed to sparkle, shine and glimmer.**

As Billy looked around
at all the colors in their glory,
he felt like he was walking through
a children's picture story.

**Then Billy came upon a leaf
that was on the water's edge.
It was so soft and fluffy,
it felt just like Billy's bed.**

So Billy laid down on the leaf
and then soon fell fast asleep.
Then the water carried him away
without so much as a peep.

**Billy dreamed of all the colors
that he saw throughout the day,
and as Billy Bee was dreaming,
he floated oh so far away.**

10

He floated far across the water;
and as his leaf washed up on shore,
Billy knew without a doubt,
that he was never there before.

The sun had gone down long ago,
and the blue sky now was night.
He was all alone and far from home
and no one was in sight.

So Billy started walking
from the beach into the trees,
but it was so dark and scary,
he was shaking at his knees.

13

Everywhere he looked,
he thought he saw a scary face.
He felt like eyes were watching him
and they were all around this place.

With the moonlight's glow behind him,
he could barely see the way;
but he knew he must keep moving on---
this was not the place to stay.

With every step he took,
a twig would snap and break,
the leaves would crunch, the wind would howl,
the more his knees would shake.

"Oh I am so scared;
I want to go back home!"
Then someone said, "I'll help you, Billy;
you're really not alone."

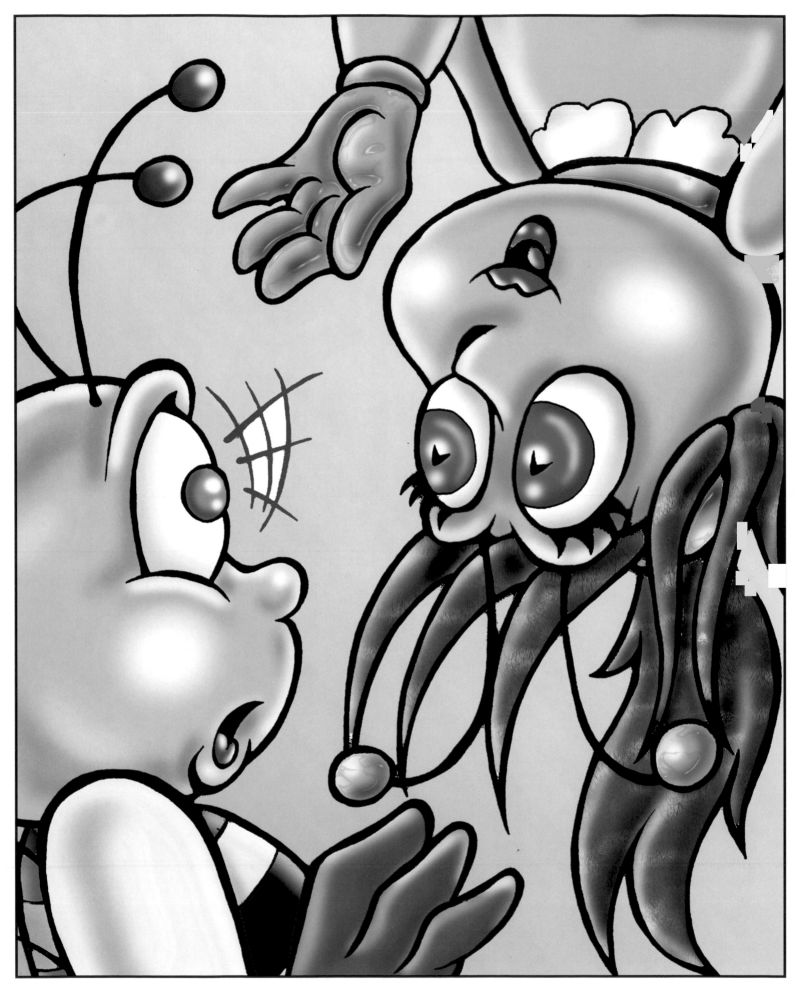

**Then Billy Bee looked up,
and much to his surprise,
there was a very pretty girl;
she was pink with big brown eyes.**

18

"Hi, my name is Jolly Jillie,"
and then she smiled wide.
Her skin was softly glowing
and Billy felt so good inside.

"I think that I can help you
to find your way back home,
but first you must believe in me
and all that you'll be shown."

So Jillie took him by the hand
and this made Billy feel so glad.
He felt like he was walking with
the best friend he ever had.

So Jillie brought him to a place
where different colors filled the night.
"This is where I live," she said.
"In the Land of Rainbow Light."

**The place was shining like a diamond,
and its beauty made you shiver
and all around the city,
ran a different colored river.**

When they came upon the city
and the gates flew open wide,
Billy Bee could not believe
the sights he saw inside.

A girl was blowing bubbles
and the tall one held balloons.
Jillie's mom was making cookies
while the music man played tunes.

There was excitement everywhere,
filled with fun and such surprise,
as a peddled helicopter
dropped some flowers from the sky.

Everyone was oh so different,
they had differences galore;
many sizes, brilliant colors,
a sight that Billy saw before.

There were purple ones and green ones,
some were pink and some were blue,
there were red ones, black and white ones,
some were striped and spotted, too.

28

"Don't be too surprised," said Jillie,
"for the best has yet to come.
Now follow me, we'll take you home,
with the help from everyone."

29

So Billy Bee and Jillie
went down to the river's shore,
but the water was a color
Billy never saw before.

Jillie told him it was emerald green
and this is where they must begin,
then she took him by the hand,
and together everyone jumped in.

He saw they all were smiling
as they were standing in the stream;
Billy Bee could not believe
all the things that he was seeing.

All their color washed right off,
the water turned pink and green and blue,
but their skin, it had no color,
and you could almost see right through.

And as Billy looked at Jillie,
with her pretty big brown eyes,
he could see right through her skin
that she was filled with love inside.

They all were filled with love.
That's what life's beauty is all about;
for when you really love someone,
it's from the inside out.

Then they started splashing,
they were playing in the stream
and the water all around them
seemed to sparkle, shine and gleam.

Then the water started bubbling
and the colors turned to light;
a rainbow blazed up through the sky.
It was the most amazing sight.

They said, "that's how we make the rainbows
that you see up in the sky.
When we wash off all our color here,
the love inside us makes it fly.

38

**At the end of every rainbow
and all the stories you've been told,
now you know they hold a treasure
worth far much more than gold."**

"This love that makes the rainbows
and all that you've been shown
is the love you have inside you
and this love will take you home."

"So close your eyes now Billy Bee,
for we must say goodbye,
but remember me and all you've seen
when there's a rainbow in the sky."

So Billy laid down on the leaf
and he swam into the light.
Then the rainbow picked up Billy Bee
and he floated out of sight.

And as Billy Bee was floating,
floating oh so far away,
the words that came to Billy's head
were all that he could say:

"A BIZZ, A BUZZ, A BEEZ, A BAMM
I'M BILLY BEE, I AM, I AM!
I CAN DO ANYTHING, I KNOW I CAN,
BECAUSE I'M BILLY BEE, I AM, I AM!"

44

When Billy opened up his eyes,
he was back home on the shore.
His Dad was saying, "Wake up, Billy;
you've been dreaming, that's for sure."

Billy said, "Oh Dad, please don't tell me
that this all was just a dream."
And Dad said, "Oh my Billy Bee,
things aren't always what they seem.

When you close your eyes and dream,
it will all be up to you;
for somewhere now inside your mind,
your dreams may all be true."

**Then they started walking home
and Billy looked up to his surprise,
they were standing underneath a rainbow
that had two pretty big brown eyes!**

**The End
or The Beginning.
Whichever you prefer.**

For More Information Call
1-(888)-BILLYBEE
245-5923
Or Go To
www.billybee.net
Thanks For BEElieving !!!